About the Author

Before internet, cellphones, social media and computers, Jareth Bramblewick grew up wandering the piney woods and creeks of North Florida, where quiet afternoons and curious creatures first sparked his imagination. Eventually, his journey carried him far from the warm, wild backcountry to the rocky coast of Camden, Maine, a place that stole his heart with its salty sea breeze, mossy forests, and working harbor boats.

In Camden, Jareth found a rhythm of life that echoed with wonder. He explored the whispering waters of the Megunticook River, played ice golf across Chickawaukie Pond, and rode the ferry from Rockland to North Haven and Vinalhaven, where spruce-scented air met the open sea. It was here, along Maine's misty shores and shadowed woodland paths, that his love for nature deepened and bloomed into story.

Today, Jareth Bramblewick writes imaginative tales for children and adults of all ages, weaving together the magic of the natural world with the quiet courage of characters who journey through it. His books carry the scent of briny winds and forest rain, and his words invite young readers to look closer, listen longer, and believe in the wild beauty of the world.

2025 Jareth Bramblewick
United States of America
IBSN: 979-8-9991260-2-3
Library of Congress Control Number: 2025920692

Megunticook Lake
TS TURN
Camden Hill State Park
MELVIN HEIGHTS
Camden
EST ROCKPORT
Rockport
Lilly Pond
1
ROCKVILLE
Chickie
Lake

Chapter 1
Life around Lilly Pond

Eliana had never really thought about how far the world stretched beyond Lilly Pond. She didn't need to. Everything that mattered was already here. Her family had lived along the edge of the pond for as long as anyone could remember. Their home was a little place tucked into the hollow of a maple tree near the old stone fence, which itself ran parallel to the path leading up to the farm.

Some said the maple tree had sheltered her great grandmother through the Great Ice Storm of 1998. Others said that her grandfather once outran a fox from the very roots of that trunk to the tangled brush by the marsh.

Eliana loved to hear about those stories. They made her feel as though she had always been part of their world. It was as if this place, the mossy stones, the cattails swaying in the breeze, the hum of frogs at night, was stitched into her fur.

Most evenings, she'd sit on the smooth rock at the pond's edge, the rock that caught the last bit of light before the sun slipped behind the ridge. And often, just as the sky turned the color of soft peaches and lavender, a familiar shadow would glide overhead.

Oscar.

He was a young osprey, maybe just a season older than her. Big, sharp eyed, always looking like he knew more than he let on. But gentle too. He'd circle once or twice before landing in the crooked pine across the water, then swoop down near her stone perch with a rustle of wings and a gust of wind that always made her fur stand on end.

"Catch anything?" she'd ask, even if he hadn't gone hunting.

"Couple of alewives," he'd shrug, fluffing his feathers. "One of them practically jumped into my talons."

Eliana would laugh. She never really knew if his stories were true, but they were always told with such ease, such wonder, that it didn't matter. She enjoyed listening to him talk about the harbor, the salt spray, the silver flashes beneath the surface. It all felt larger than life.

Her world, in contrast, was quiet and gentle. She knew every bend of the Lilly Pond trail and every crack in the stone wall that encircled the old Seaview Cemetery down the lane.

The cemetery wasn't spooky the way some might think. It was beautiful and peaceful and impeccably well kept, with tidy rows of headstones, scattered towering oaks, and flowers that seemed to bloom even when nothing else dared to.

Eliana's parents would sometimes take her there on slow afternoons. Her mother would point out the names on the stones, telling her stories of the lives they might have lived. A man who once carved boats from driftwood. A boy who loved skipping stones across the pond, just like Eliana loved to do.

She'd listen, nodding, imagining the lives of these people as threads weaving through her own. It was a simple life. Steady and predictable.

But now and then, when Oscar spoke of the sun setting over Camden Harbor, or of the scent of mackerel in the air near Rockport Harbor, something tugged quietly inside her. It was like curiosity gently waking up.

You ever wonder what's out there?" Oscar asked one evening, from his perch up in a tree. He motioned with his wing toward the horizon. Eliana squinted into the distance. "Out where?"

"Just . . . out. Beyond the pond. Past the hill. All the way to the ocean." Eliana thought for a moment, then shrugged. "I dunno. Seems like a long way to go just to get your feathers wet." He chuckled. "Maybe. But it's something."

Eliana looked up at him in the overhanging tree. He was silhouetted against the fading sky, feathers catching the gold of the setting sun. For the first time, she realized just how far he could see from up there. How much more he must know.

The pond rippled quietly below. A bat flitted past, chasing down the night's first mosquitoes. Somewhere in the reeds, a bullfrog croaked its low, lazy tune. And Eliana, small and warm in the cooling air, sat there on the stone. She was starting to wonder what it might feel like to see her world from above. And in that moment, she knew her story was about to change.

Chapter 2
Sunsets and Big Dreams

Oscar always had a way of arriving without a sound. Eliana would be curled up on the big flat stone by the pond, nibbling on a hazelnut or just listening to the breeze rustling through the reeds, when suddenly there'd be a soft gust of wind and a gentle thud behind her. And there he would be, Oscar the Osprey, tall and feathered, standing with the sort of presence of a watchful guardian, alert, composed, and aware of everything the world had to offer.

"I didn't hear you coming," Eliana said one evening. She did not bother to look up from where she was perched, watching the sky turn orange. "You never do," he replied, grinning the way birds do, with a tilt of the head and a gleam in the eye.

He settled beside her, wings folded in, talons tucked under. It was their ritual now, these quiet evenings on the stone, watching the pond go still and the sky slip into its softer colors. Bats zipped overhead in little flickers, zigzagging through the air with purpose only they seemed to understand.

"They're like dancers," Eliana said.

Oscar followed her gaze. "Or drunk acrobats."

She laughed, short and surprised. "That's not very poetic."

"Neither is being eaten alive by mosquitoes."

They sat in the comfortable silence that only exists between friends who've known each other for a long time. The sun dipped lower, and the clouds caught fire with the last bits of daylight. Eliana turned to him. "Tell me more, what's it like out there?"

Oscar glanced down at her.

"You know. The places you go. Camden Harbor. Penobscot Bay. Rockport Harbor. All of it."

He was quiet for a beat, like he wasn't sure how to begin. "It's . . . open," he said finally. "You feel the wind under your wings, and it's like the whole world is breathing with you. Boats dotting the water. Fish darting below, sometimes in huge shimmering schools. Seals sunning on rocks. Once I flew alongside a bald eagle for nearly a mile. Didn't say a word. Just flew."

Eliana watched him as he spoke. His voice always changed when he talked about flying, it got lighter, as if even the memory of it lifted him a little. "It sounds beautiful," she said.

"It is," he answered, nodding. "It's more than that. It's . . . wild. There's no map. You just go."

She looked out over the pond again. The cattails stood like sentinels. The surface of the water reflected the last streaks of daylight, broken only by soft rings where a frog had jumped in. "I've never gone anywhere," Eliana said quietly. "I mean, I've been down to the cemetery. There, I know every curve in the stone wall, every flower bed."

"That place with the tulips and the little gate that sticks?" he asked.

"Yeah," she said, smiling. "That's the one."

Oscar didn't say anything for a while. He just watched the bats dance across the deepening blue.

PATH
to
HARBOR

Eliana hadn't wondered about what was past the cemetery. Not until recently. Not until Oscar had started painting these pictures of harbors and the sky and the shimmer of fish in sunlit water.

"Sometimes I think about it," she said. "But I like it here. It's familiar and comfortable and safe."

Oscar gave a soft, thoughtful hum. "Yeah. But sometimes the best views come when you're a little bit off the map."

She chuckled at that. "That sounds like something a bird would say."

"Guilty."

The stars were coming out now, scattered like fireflies above the darkening pond. One blinked. Then another. Oscar stood, stretching his wings. "I've got an idea," he said, in that casual way of his that always made her suspicious that something big was coming.

"Oh no," she said, narrowing her eyes. "I know that tone."

"I'm serious. Just think about it."

"Think about what?"

He turned, feathers catching the moonlight. "What if you didn't have to wonder what was out there? What if I showed you?"

Eliana sat up slowly. "You mean . . . fly? With you?"

Oscar gave a small nod.

"But I'm a chipmunk, Oscar. We don't fly."

"Not on your own, no. But I've got wings and you've got curiosity."

She stared at him. The idea felt ridiculous. Impossible. And yet, it sparked something. A little thrill. A little fear. Both at the same time. "I don't know," Eliana said honestly. "That's a big ask."

He smiled again, though not in a pushy way. Just warm. Patient. "No rush," he said. "The sky'll still be there when you're ready." And with that, he launched into the air, silent and strong, rising into the night sky.

Eliana watched until she couldn't see him anymore. The pond was quiet again.

The moon peeked up and sprinkled silver over the water, and in the stillness, she felt something new and beautiful wake inside her.

It was a morning that felt like a secret. The pond was unusually still, like it had paused in mid breath. The light spilling through the trees was that soft kind you only get for a few minutes after sunrise, when everything touched by it looks a little more golden and a little more alive.

Eliana had been up since just before dawn. She woke up, wide-eyed and alert, with something electric running through her. Like the world had whispered. She sat by the water's edge, stoically perched and listening to the quiet chirr of dragonflies skating across the lily pads. Her siblings were still curled up back in the den. The morning dew hadn't yet burned off the leaves.

Then, there it was. The soft swoop of wings. Oscar landed nearby with the grace of someone who's done it a thousand times but still enjoys the landing. He was carrying something in his beak, a leaf wrapped parcel, slightly damp. "For you," he said, dropping it beside her with a clumsy sort of pride.

Eliana blinked at it. "What is it?"

He nudged it open. Inside were three tiny mackerel scales, a smooth piece of blue sea glass the color of fog, and a single downy feather from a loon.

Eliana tilted her head. "You brought me… ocean things?"

Oscar smiled. "Well, technically I brought you a starter kit. For adventure."

She laughed. "That's not a real thing."

"It is now," he said. "You've got curiosity. All you need is a little push."

She looked out at the water, at the reflection of the trees and sky. Everything felt suddenly still again, like the moment was still holding its breath.

"Eliana," Oscar said with excitement. "Let me show you."

She didn't answer right away. She looked down at her paws and then up at his wings, folded so easily along his sides. It all seemed so simple for him. For her, the world was tangled roots and narrow paths. Safety in corners. Life lived close to the ground. "I don't even know how," she admitted. "What do I do? Hold on to your neck?"

Oscar chuckled. "No. That'd mess with my feathers. Just climb on. Settle between the shoulder blades. I'll stay steady."

Eliana hesitated. "You sure I won't fall?"

"I've swooped up fish heavier than you," he teased with a glint in his eye. "You're like a peanut with a tail!"

She narrowed her eyes. "Wow. So flattering."

He smiled and then turned slightly, angling his back toward her.

She stood up slowly, heart beating a little faster now. Climbing on was awkward. She had to adjust her paws, shift her weight, and try not to grip too tightly. Oscar waited patiently, making small adjustments, wings twitching once or twice to keep balance. Once she was in place, she exhaled. "Okay."

"You ready?"

"No."

He took off anyway.

The ground fell away beneath them in a rush of wind and light. Eliana gasped from sheer impossible wonder. The trees spread out like veins on a maple leaf, the pond became a coin of silver in the sun, and the farm fields in the distance glowed in long, morning shadows.

They circled Lilly Pond once, Oscar keeping low and wide. Eliana clung tight at first, heart in her throat. But the longer they stayed up, the more the fear faded. "This is insaaaaane!" she shouted over the wind.

Oscar only laughed. They passed over Aldermere Farm, the Belted Galloway cows below dotting the field like little spilled chocolates.

Then they climbed higher. The air was cooler now and the wind stronger. There was Camden up ahead, with houses tucked among trees, boats nestled in the harbor like toys, and the ocean beyond stretching towards the sky.

Eliana went quiet. All that she knew, her favorite tree, the stone wall at the cemetery, looked so small now.

Oscar tilted a wing, circling gently. "You good back there?" he called.

She blinked. "Yeah. I'm… I'm really good!"

They flew on, and as the light caught the tips of Oscar's wings, Eliana thought to herself, today really was different!

For a little while, Eliana couldn't speak. She just held on and let the world unfold beneath her. The wind pressed against her fur, tugged at her ears, and filled her lungs with a kind of crispness she'd never known. Everything was moving. From her heart to the trees below, it felt amazing.

They flew over the edge of Lilly Pond again. This time, Eliana saw it from even higher above, and it was not just the still water she'd known since she was small. Now she saw the shaded shallows near the reeds, and the cluster of lily pads like green coin shaped islands. She even spotted the crooked pine near her family's tree, the one that always leaned a little left after a winter storm a few years back.

It was funny how different things looked when you rose above them.

"Still with me?" Oscar called, angling one wing slightly as they started to climb.

"Yeah," Eliana called, but her voice came out thin, almost like it didn't want to interrupt the view. Below them, the landscape slowly stretched out. The gentle sloping hills gave way to the grid of town roads.

And then, all at once, the world opened up. Camden Harbor and Penobscot Bay seemed to go on forever.

Oscar slowed, catching a thermal that held them aloft like an invisible hand. They drifted quietly over the rooftops, the old library, the white steepled church, and finally out toward the water. Boats rocked gently in their slips. Masts pointed skyward like quills in a giant inkwell. People walked along the docks, but from this height, they looked like tiny ants, just small lives going about their day.

And there were the fish. "Look down," Oscar said, tilting his head just enough for her to follow his gaze. Beneath the surface, schools of mackerel moved like liquid silver. They swirled in tight shimmering patterns near the pier and were followed by schools of giant striped bass scooping up mackerel one at a time.

Eliana's mouth fell open a little. She hadn't realized how clearly you could see through the water from above. "Do you always see this?" she asked, her voice soft.

"Not always," Oscar said. "Some days the wind's too rough. Some days the water's cloudy. But on mornings like this? Yeah. This is what I see."

They floated a little longer, gliding past the rocky edge near the Megunticook River. Oscar pointed out the spillway, where the water rushed down in a foamy white torrent. To Eliana, it looked like the edge of the world.

She clung tighter as he dipped low, skimming just above the treetops that framed the river. "Okay," she called out, voice half laughing now. "I get why you never sit still!"

Oscar grinned. "Told you."

Then a sudden flash of white streaked past them from the left. There was another from the right. Eliana squeaked and ducked instinctively, pressing herself flat against Oscar's back.

"Whoa, hey!" Oscar flared his wings, hovering in place.

Two seagulls circled back, wings wide and flapping hard. "Hey!" the first

gull called, his tone somewhere between confused and suspicious. "Is that a chipmunk on your back?"

Eliana peeked out cautiously. "Uh . . . hi?"

Oscar gave a quick flap, stabilizing them in the air. "She's with me."
The second gull tilted its head. "That's not something you see every day."
"Looked like a rescue mission at first," the first one added. "Thought maybe she got picked up by accident."

"I volunteered," Eliana said, raising her paw like it was roll call at school.

The gulls blinked, and then looked at each other, and laughed. "Well, in that case," the first gull said, "carry on."

"Thanks for the air escort, gentlemen," Oscar said. The two gulls nodded and veered off, still chuckling, and Oscar shook his head. "Seagulls," he muttered.

"They weren't wrong," Eliana said, smirking. "It is a strange sight."

"Maybe," he said. "But you're handling it better than most squirrels I know."

"I'm not a squirrel."

Oscar glanced back. "Exactly."

They glided toward Rockport next, hugging the coastline. The cliffs dropped dramatically into the water, and the sea below glimmered in sunlit

streaks. Waves slapped gently against the boulders with a quiet rhythm. Farther out, a few lobster boats bobbed in the swell, and red buoys dotted the sea like forgotten berries.

Eliana leaned into the curve as Oscar dipped low again, flying just above the waves. The scent of salt filled her nose and the ocean mist clung to her fur. It was exhilarating! She wanted to bottle the feeling and carry it in her chest forever.

Then, as if summoned by the hush that comes right before something ends, the sun began to slide down into the far edge of the sky. The clouds turned orange and pink, and then faded into a sleepy lavender.

"We should head back," Oscar said, his voice a little quieter now.

Eliana didn't argue. She just nodded, taking one last look at the horizon. They turned inland, climbing gently, and traced the path back to Lilly Pond.

When they landed, the sky was darkening fast. Crickets had already started their evening chorus and the spring peepers were joining in.

Oscar crouched low in the grass to let her off. Eliana slid down his back and stood for a moment, wobbling just slightly as her paws remembered what it felt like to be on solid ground.

"Well?" he asked.

She looked at him, still catching her breath. "I don't even have words."

He nodded, like he understood.

The den in the hollow of the maple tree was not far away. Eliana could hear her younger siblings chattering, their voices rising and falling like songbirds. Her mother was still setting out the dandelion greens she had harvested earlier in the day. Her father sat sharpening a piece of bark into a walking stick.

She turned back toward Oscar. "Thank you."

"Anytime," he said. "Really." He gave a small nod and launched into the air again, climbing fast until he disappeared beyond the canopy. Eliana stood for a while, paws still tingling and heart still racing. Tonight, she wouldn't fall asleep easily. But for once, that didn't feel like a problem.

By now, Eliana was getting used to the feeling of air beneath her. Not that it wasn't still completely wild, because it was. Every time Oscar's wings lifted them into the sky, her stomach did this flip that she hadn't yet decided she liked.

But there was something else now, too. A quiet kind of trust. Like leaning into the wind and letting go of the need to know exactly where you'd land.

On this particular day, they had just crossed over the edge of Camden Harbor again. Oscar glided effortlessly, the tips of his wings adjusting with each little shift of the breeze. Below them, the water shimmered like a bowl of light, and the masts of the sailboats traced long shadows across the docks.

Eliana sat perched between his wings, tucked low, paws wrapped around a small tuft of feathers. "I can see fish again," she called out, trying to be heard over the wind.

Oscar banked gently to the left. "Told you they love this corner of the harbor."

She watched a school of something silvery move in one perfect motion, all turning at once like a thought. "Why do they do that?" she asked.

Oscar glanced back. "Stick together, stay alive. That's kind of the fish motto."
"I like that," Eliana said. "Simple and true."

They floated in silence for a few moments longer, just drifting. The harbor curved around them like an open palm, boats bobbing gently and flags fluttering from riggings.

Then, just ahead, two shapes cut through the air fast and sharp. Big birds coming in from opposite sides. Pelicans.

There was an awkward pause, like the air itself was trying to decide what to do next. Then a scratchy voiced pelican broke into a laugh. "Well, I'll be! Haven't seen anything like that since the pelican gave a ride to the turtle." "That was different," the other one muttered.

Oscar rolled his eyes. "Look, we're just flying. She wanted to see the coast."

"Hey, no judgment," the first pelican said. "Just unexpected. We usually only see osprey hauling mackerel."

Oscar smirked. "She's lighter than a mackerel." Eliana frowned. "I am right here, you know!"

The pelicans both laughed, their sharp voices echoing over the harbor. "Fair enough," said the scratchy one. "Well, carry on, you two. You heading toward Rockport?"

"Thinking about it," Oscar said.

"We'll fly with you a bit," the pelican added. "Make sure no one else freaks out." And just like that, they had company.

Eliana loosened her grip a little and sat taller. The initial panic had passed, and now she was just amused. Grateful, too. The pelicans hadn't meant any harm, they'd just never seen anything like her and Oscar before. It made sense. "Are you always this dramatic?" she asked, leaning toward Oscar.

"I prefer the term 'memorable'," he replied, banking slightly to avoid a gust of wind.

The pelicans flew a bit ahead now, calling to each other over the sound of the sea below. From time to time, they'd glance back, still curious and slightly bewildered. But Eliana didn't mind. Let them look. Let the whole sky wonder.

She was flying.

They left the pelicans behind somewhere near the edge of Rockport Harbor, where the docks gave way to rougher stones and the wind carried the scent of salt and seaweed in equal measure.

Oscar dipped low, catching an updraft and then skimming just above the waves.

Eliana leaned forward, squinting against the breeze, ears flattened back and heart racing in the best way. The ocean was right there below them, so close she could hear it breathing.

Waves curled and uncurled like sleeping giants, their white crests catching the sunlight. Every now and then, a patch of kelp floated by, swaying just beneath the surface like a collection of underwater flags. And in the distance, a cormorant dove headfirst, disappearing in a blink.

Oscar tilted his wings slightly as he continued flying only a few feet above the water. Eliana gripped a little tighter. "You're not trying to make me nervous, right?" she called out, half laughing.

Oscar's voice drifted back, calm and confident. "Nope. Just showing you the good stuff."

Eliana grinned. This, this was the good stuff!

They soared along the rocky shoreline, past weathered boathouses and over tiny beaches that were only visible at low tide. A couple of harbor seals popped their heads above the water as they passed, blinking up at them like sleepy beachgoers not quite ready to be noticed.

Eliana couldn't stop staring. Everything was in motion, from the waves to the light skipping across the water. Even the wind seemed to have its own rhythm, brushing past her with every rise and fall. It felt like the ocean was putting on a dance and she was the audience. Or maybe even a small part of the performance.

Oscar climbed again, banking toward the harbor. "See that big red buoy?" he asked. "I used to perch there when I was younger. Thought it made me look important."

"Did it?" asked Eliana. "I mean . . . maybe you looked important to the lobsters."

They continued around the outer edge of Rockport Harbor, where tiny boats lay anchored in a lazy scatter. A few seabirds called out from a piling. A person below pointed upward, though Eliana couldn't tell if it was at them or just at the sky.

"It's beautiful," she said quietly.

Oscar glanced back. "Yeah. It really is."

They hovered for a moment above the channel, letting the wind do most of the work. The sun was still bright, but the shadows were starting to stretch just a little. That golden late afternoon feeling was beginning to settle over everything.

"I used to think Lilly Pond was the whole world," Eliana murmured, almost to herself. "And it was, in a way. Everything I knew was there."

Oscar said nothing. He just continued flying and let her speak.

HARBOR MASTER

"But now . . . this?" She looked around at the cliffs, the water, and the stretch of sky. "I didn't know how much I didn't know."

Oscar finally spoke. "That's the best part about flying. It doesn't change where you're from. It just reminds you that there's more."

They flew a little longer, with no particular destination in mind. Just movement. Just the quiet thrill of existing in a wider world than yesterday.

Eventually, the sun began to slip toward the horizon, brushing the clouds with warm, sleepy hues. The breeze cooled. Even the waves seemed to settle into a slower rhythm.

"Time to head back?" Oscar asked.

Eliana nodded, though part of her wanted to keep going. Just a little farther. Just a few more minutes. But she knew you couldn't outrun the setting sun. And part of the magic, she figured, was knowing when to turn back so you could carry all of it home.

As they made their way inland, Eliana looked down one last time. The ocean was still dancing. Just for her.

By the time they neared the edge of town again, the sun had slipped behind the hills and left the sky glowing in soft watercolor hues. There was amber bleeding into lavender, with the faintest brush of blue still clinging to the edges. The lights along the harbor blinked on one by one, their reflections stretching long and thin across the water like threads.

Eliana had gone quiet. She was feeling the soft ache of knowing a moment is ending, and already missing it while still in the moment.

Oscar didn't say much, either. He just flew. Steady and smooth, gliding on muscle memory now, as if he knew the way home by heart.

Below them, the familiar curves of Camden began to reappear. There was Beach Hill in the distance, its rooftops nestled between the trees, and the little stream that traced its way back toward the pond like a silver ribbon.

Then, finally, there it was, Lilly Pond. Small, serene, and entirely unchanged. The cattails swaying at the far end. The smooth flat rock where she'd first sat with Oscar and listened to him talk about the world beyond. It was all there, just as Eliana had left it, and yet it was funny how something so familiar could suddenly feel so different.

Oscar dipped lower and let the treetops rise up around them like a cradle. As they approached the clearing, he slowed to a hover, flapping just enough to stay steady, and then, with the lightest touch, he landed.

Eliana clambered off his back. Her legs were a little shaky, and her paws were tingling. "That was . . . ," she started to say, but she didn't finish. She didn't need to.

Oscar just nodded. "I know."

She looked around. Fireflies had started to appear, blinking in and out like tiny stars. Her younger siblings were rustling around near the den as they chased each other in figure eights. She could hear her mother's voice in the distance, calling someone in for supper.

Eliana stood still for a moment, not quite ready to rejoin it all.

"You okay?" Oscar asked.

She turned to him. "Yeah."

Oscar let out a soft chuckle.

They stood together, not saying much. The pond lapped gently at the shore.

Somewhere in the distance, a loon let out its strange, mournful cry.

Eliana finally exhaled and said, "Thank you."

Oscar tilted his head. "For what?"

"For carrying me. For sharing it. For not letting me stay small."

He gave a quiet nod, wings folding in at his sides. "You were never small." She looked up at him, surprised.

"You just hadn't seen yourself from the sky yet." For a moment, Oscar's words hung there, soft and true.

Then came the sound of her siblings calling her name, shouting it in that breathless, excited way that only children can shout, like every word might tumble out of their mouths if they don't say them fast enough. "Eliana! Eliana! Did you fly? Where did you go this time? Did you see the ocean?"

She turned toward them and smiled, suddenly feeling very ready to talk. To tell. To relive it all.

Oscar spread his wings again, ready to head toward his nest.

"Will I see you tomorrow?" Eliana asked.

"Probably," he said. "If the wind's good." He took off with a beat of his wings and disappeared into the darkening trees, heading for the old pine he called home.

Eliana stood for another second, watching the stars come out. Then she turned and ran toward her family, words already spilling from her, words like harbor and fish and sky. The world was bigger now. And so was she.

Eliana didn't sleep much that night. She tried, curled up in her usual spot, with the soft hum of crickets just outside the burrow and the quiet warmth of her siblings nearby.

But her mind was still flying. In her thoughts, she was still riding the currents, still tracing the coastline, still hearing the rush of the wind and the laughter of gulls and the distant splash of ocean water below. When the first light of dawn slipped in through the branches, painting the walls of the burrow in faint amber, she was already awake.

Oscar showed up just after sunrise, always punctual.

He landed beside her tree with a soft thump and shook out his feathers, scattering a little dew from the early flight. "You're up early," he said, eyeing her with that knowing look.

Eliana nodded. "Didn't sleep much."

"Nerves?"

"No," she said. Then paused. "Maybe a little. But mostly... I didn't want to forget anything."

Oscar smiled. "That's a good reason."

She'd come prepared this time. A little bundle of nuts and seeds tied in a leaf pouch, slung across her back with a strand of grass like a satchel. She'd packed it carefully, walnuts for protein, sunflower seeds for energy, and just a few dried blueberries because they made her happy.

Her parents were half awake, blinking at her with equal parts pride and worry. "Be careful," her mother had whispered, pressing her nose to Eliana's cheek. "Stay close to Oscar."

Eliana had nodded. "I always do."

Now she was climbing onto his back again, paws steady, heart surprisingly calm. It wasn't like the first time. The flutter was still there, but it was less about fear and more about anticipation. "Where are we going?" she asked as he lifted off.

"Chickie Lake," Oscar said, adjusting his flight path as they climbed. "It's further inland. Bigger than Lilly Pond. Wilder, too. It's where I go when I want to fish without all the noise."

Eliana settled into the rhythm of his flight, the wind already brushing her face. They passed over Camden again, but this time she saw it differently. It was less like a city and more like a memory, something she'd already tucked into her heart.

Then came Rockport. The harbor looked sleepy this early in the morning, it hadn't quite decided to wake up yet. The sun crept higher as they veered west, following the winding edge of the hills. Below them, trees thickened and roads thinned out. The world began to feel more like forest.

Eliana pointed with one paw. "What's that?"

Oscar glanced down. "That's the stone house on Beach Hill. Built over a hundred years ago for a family to use as a picnic spot." Eliana's eyes widened. "It looks like something from a fairy tale."

Oscar laughed. "Wait until you see the lake."

It took them a while to get to the lake, long enough for Eliana to finish half her pouch and start feeling the pleasant ache of travel. But when Chickie Lake came into view, it really did take her breath away.

It was massive. Much bigger than anything she'd expected. Long and winding, with fingers of water stretching between rocky ridges and patches of pine forest. The surface glittered in the sunlight like someone had spilled stars across it.

Oscar swooped lower, skimming the surface before angling up again. "Told you," he said.

They landed near a rocky bluff that jutted out above the water, a natural lookout spot that Oscar apparently knew well. She hopped down, stretching her legs and shaking out the travel jitters. The air smelled different here, cleaner, sharper, like pine needles and lake water and something just a little bit wild.

Oscar stood beside her, folding his wings. "You okay?"

Eliana nodded slowly. "I didn't think it could get better than yesterday."

"It usually does," he said. "If you keep looking."

They sat in a comfortable silence, watching the ripples roll out across the lake. Loons called in the distance, low and eerie and beautiful. Dragonflies hovered in lazy zigzags near the reeds.

Then Eliana froze. "Wait. Did you hear that?"

RIVERHOUSE
FOOTBRIDGE 1953
Caution
Slipery
When
Icy

Oscar perked up. "Hear what?"

"That." It was faint but unmistakable: a series of small, quick chirps from the trees just behind them.

She turned around, ears up. More chipmunks! Three of them, staring wide-eyed from the underbrush. One whispered something to the others, and suddenly they all scattered, leaping onto branches and ducking behind rocks.

Oscar shifted uneasily. "Should I go?"

Eliana turned to him. "No. Wait here." She hopped forward slowly, paws raised, voice calm. "It's okay! He's with me!"

The chipmunks peeked out, still wary.

"He's not hunting," she said. "He's my friend."

There was a long pause. Then a smaller chipmunk with a crooked stripe down his back stepped forward. "Friends with an osprey?" he asked.

Eliana smiled. "It's a long story.

The new chipmunks all crept out, little by little. She told them about Lilly Pond, about Camden Harbor, about the first flight and the seagulls and the ocean.

Their eyes grew wider with every word. One of them, a girl named Poppy, clapped her paws together. "I didn't know there were other chipmunks out there!" "Neither did I," Eliana said.

HEMINGWAY
ROCKPORT ME

They all turned to look at Oscar. He stood a little awkwardly at the edge of the clearing, trying not to look too large or too talon-y.

Eventually, Poppy took a few steps forward. "Hi," she said.

Oscar dipped his head. "Hi."

And just like that, curiosity bloomed. Questions tumbled out. "Where do you live? What's it like to fly? What does ocean water taste like?"

Eliana leaned back, watching as two small worlds began to weave themselves into one. Before she knew it, morning had melted into afternoon, and the whole day had slipped by in laughter and play.

Later, when the sun was starting to drift again and Oscar said it was time to go, Poppy and the others walked Eliana back to the bluff. "Will you come back?" one of them asked.

Eliana looked at Oscar, who nodded. "Yeah," she said. "I think I will."

As they rose into the sky, she glanced down at the lake, her new friends, the trees, and for the first time, she didn't feel like a visitor at all. She felt like a bridge between them.

The wind was soft this morning, one of those gentle breezes that doesn't really push or pull but just lets you coast. Oscar let it carry them for a while, wings outstretched like sails.

Eliana nestled between his shoulders, her little satchel tucked under one paw and her head resting on the other. She wasn't tired, she was full of questions, new names, new smells. Loons calling across still water, the faces of chipmunks who looked like cousins but felt like strangers. And of the way the wind sounded different over Chickie Lake, like it had a story of its own.

"You okay back there?" Oscar called, without looking back.

"Yeah," she said, and then paused. "Actually, no. I don't know. I think I'm overwhelmed."

Oscar chuckled. "That's not always a bad thing."

"I don't think it is," she said. "But my brain's definitely trying to keep up."

He banked slightly, steering toward a long granite outcrop that overlooked the western edge of Megunticook Lake. "Let's land up here," he said. "It's quiet."

Soon Oscar touched down lightly, with the practiced grace. Eliana got down from the his back with a little hop.

The cliff was wide and sun warmed, with a patch of soft moss at one end and just enough elevation to see the lake stretch for miles. The sun was lower now and cast everything in golden layers. Megunticook glittered below them, calm and endless.

Eliana wandered to the edge and looked out. A loon cried again, its voice echoing down the hills.

Oscar settled beside her, folding his wings with a rustle.

"You come here often?" she asked.

He nodded. "When I want to think. Or not think," he said with a chuckle.

They sat in a long, easy silence for a time. And then, out of the quiet, there was a faint rustle behind them.

Eliana turned fast, ears twitching. Three small chipmunks stood frozen near the tree line, and they were not the ones from yesterday. These were younger. Curious. Eyes wide.

Oscar stiffened slightly.

These chipmunks didn't run or try to hide. They just watched, shifting their weight and whispering to each other with those rapid little chirps only chipmunks can make.

One of them, a sandy furred girl with bright eyes, stepped forward. "Is he with you?" she asked, nodding at Oscar.

Eliana smiled. "He is."

"Are you safe?"

Eliana laughed, soft and warm. "Safer than I've ever been."

More rustling. A few more chipmunks appeared, drawn by the commotion. Eliana counted seven in total, their little faces tilted in wonder and their noses twitching like they were trying to sniff out the truth.

"Everyone," she said, standing up a little straighter. "This is Oscar. He's my friend."

The youngest one piped up: "But he's an osprey!"

"I know," Eliana said. "And I'm a chipmunk. And usually, yeah, that wouldn't make sense." There was a hesitation in the air. "But he's never hurt me," she continued. "In fact, he's the one who's been carrying me. Showing me places I never thought I'd see."

Oscar looked slightly uncomfortable under the attention, but stayed quiet.

The girl with the bright eyes took another step forward. "That's weird."

"It is," Eliana said. "But it's also kind of wonderful."

Silence again. Then one of the older chipmunks looked at Oscar and asked, "What does it feel like to fly?"

Oscar blinked. Then, surprisingly, he answered. "Like being part of the sky," he said. "Like moving with the world instead of through it."

The chipmunks murmured among themselves. And then, one by one, they began sitting down, right there on the mossy edge of the cliff. Not running or hiding. Just listening.

FREYAS
FREYAS

Another day had flown by in a blur, and Eliana sat in wonder, amazed by how many others were out there in the world, creatures she'd never even known existed.

As the sun dipped lower and the lake water shimmered in the last light of day, Oscar and Eliana told their story of ponds and harbors, of seagulls and sailboats, of curiosity and courage, and of the strange, unexpected beauty of trusting someone very different from you.

By the time they finished, it was nearly dark. Fireflies were blinking among the ferns, and the night sounds had taken over, crickets and frogs and the gentle whisper of wind through the pines.

Eliana turned to Oscar. "I think they're starting to believe it."

"They should," he said. "It's all true."

She smiled, heart swelling again in that now familiar way.

At Lilly Pond, she had thought that the stone wall around the cemetery marked the edge of her world. But here she was now on a cliff above Megunticook Lake, surrounded by new voices and new questions.

And the wall at her home? It wasn't the edge after all.

That evening, the chipmunks finally stopped looking at Oscar like he was a shadow that might swoop. It didn't happen all at once, but it softened, like frost retreating from sunlight. A few kept their distance, though most began to lean in, curiosity replacing their nerves. The air grew warmer as the scent of pine drifted through the moss, and soon the clearing hummed with the sounds of talking, nibbling, laughing.

The little ones were first to break the spell. "Do ospreys snore?" "Can he see in the dark?" "How high can he go?" Their voices bubbled up like spring water. Oscar, to his credit, answered each question without a single sigh. Once, he even made a joke about flying backward, and the whole group squeaked in delight.

Eliana didn't try to lead. She simply sat with them, her tone calm, like a flame that didn't flicker no matter the wind. She spoke of home, of Lilly Pond's crooked pine, of bats that darted through twilight, of tulips blooming near the old cemetery wall when snow still clung to the leaves. She told them about her first flight. The fear. The wonder. The shock of how beautiful the world looked when the ground let go.

Some leaned closer, whiskers twitching, as if they could almost feel the lift beneath their paws. "You don't forget it," she said quietly. "Once you've seen that far."

One of the elders nodded. "Must be something, having a bird for a friend." "It is," she said, and she meant it.

When someone passed around dried apples and clover bundles, Oscar declined politely. The gesture itself was enough. In that small act, the invisible wall between them dissolved. By the time the stars came out, he wasn't an outsider anymore. He was part of their story.

Later, when the others began slipping into burrows and nests, Oscar stood, stretching his wings. "We should head home," he murmured. Eliana brushed crumbs from her paws, looked back once at the sleepy clearing, and nodded. Together, they glided off the cliff into a night so deep it felt like flying through velvet.

Below them, treetops shimmered with dew. Above, the stars stretched wide and old. And as they sailed toward Lilly Pond, Eliana thought about how a single "yes" could open a door she hadn't known existed. How a simple friendship could unfold into something that changed everything.

By the time they landed, morning was already spilling across the water. Mist drifted like silk over the pond's surface, the air full of light and frog song. Her siblings froze mid-step when they saw her. Then came the questions, as endless as ripples: "Did you see bears?" "Did you eat fish?" "Did the air taste like the ocean?"

Eliana laughed, catching her breath. "Oscar ate fish. I stuck with seeds." They pressed closer, eager for every word. Their father appeared at the den mouth, blinking away sleep. "You all right?" he asked.

"More than all right," she said, and he smiled.

Oscar waited near the trees, his shadow long across the grass. Eliana turned toward her family. "There are others out there," she said. "Chipmunks like us. We didn't know about them. They didn't know about us."

Her mother tilted her head, curious.

"We're not alone," Eliana said simply.

That was how the idea began. Soon there were satchels of pine nuts, bundles of dried berries, scraps of birch bark scrawled with tiny notes. Oscar carried them, wings flashing silver as he rose into the sky. When he returned with a pouch tied in a different knot and a small message that read Yes. We'd love to visit, something inside Eliana clicked into place. The world wasn't divided by ponds or trees. It was stitched together, waiting to be seen.

Weeks passed in quiet preparation. Then one bright afternoon, the visitors came. Poppy led the way, her fur dusted with travel, her brother behind her with the crooked stripe that made him easy to spot. Two others followed, faces new but eyes familiar. For a long moment, both groups just stared. The air was heavy with sun and nerves.

Then Eliana stepped forward. "Hi, Poppy."

Poppy smiled. "Hey."

That was enough. Names spilled out, laughter followed, and soon everyone was talking at once. Someone shared apple slices, another poured thistle tea into acorn cups. When the sun dropped behind the trees, chipmunks from two lakes were tangled together in the grass, swapping stories as if they'd known each other forever.

Oscar perched above on a pine branch, preening, content. When Eliana looked up, he gave a small nod. She understood what he meant. Some journeys don't end where you think they will, they just lead you higher.

As dusk folded in, songs rose from the clearing, new melodies twining with old ones. Later, when quiet returned, Eliana walked to the water's edge. The reflection of fireflies shimmered on the pond's skin.

Oscar landed softly beside her. "Busy day," he said.

"The best kind."

They watched the bats swoop low, the fireflies blink. "Do you miss the quiet?" he asked.

Eliana thought for a long time. "I used to," she said finally. "But now quiet feels like waiting. And I'm done waiting."

Oscar's feathers rustled. "There's a lake farther out," he said. "Bigger than Chickie. Hardly anyone flies over it."

She smiled. "Tomorrow?"

He grinned. "Tomorrow."

They sat together as the stars stitched across the sky, patient and bright. Eliana once believed the world ended at the stone wall near the old cemetery. But now she knew better. There were no edges. Only beginnings, and the courage to follow them.

One flight had started it all. And above them, the sky waited, wide open, unending.

Sometimes, when the wind shifts just right over Lilly Pond... when the cattails lean ever so slightly east... when the dragonflies hang still in the air... you can hear the sound of wings. The quiet rhythm of someone coming home.

Oscar still flies over most mornings. Sometimes it's just a pass overhead. A shadow flickering across the pond. A brief glint of white and brown against the sky.

But Eliana always notices. She'll pause whatever she's doing, hauling a pinecone, helping her younger siblings gather seeds, sitting on that same flat rock by the water, and she'll look up, smiling. Because even now, after everything, it still stirs the memory of knowing that she's been up there, too.

Things have changed around Lilly Pond. You'd have to be paying close attention to notice, but they have. Not only is there a new path for humans from Aldermere Farm to Lilly Pond, but there are more chipmunks from Chickie Lake and even beyond. Some come for a few days. Some stay longer.

There's a little footpath now between the pond and the woods beyond the ridge, where Eliana once thought the world ended. It's been worn smooth by paws and years and the quiet, persistent work of friendship.

And stories. So many stories. Told under starlight beside mossy stumps, while sharing nuts and dried berries. Stories of other ponds and other hills, of new birds who offer rides and of rivers that wind through forests no one's yet mapped. Eliana still tells hers sometimes, when someone new arrives. Her stories have their own kind of magic.

She always starts the same way: "I used to think the world stopped at the cemetery wall." And she always ends it the same way, too: "But then I said yes."

There's no plaque or statue or grand tale written down in the bark of the trees. But if you listen, you can feel it in the hush of the wind through the leaves, in the way the bats skim lower at dusk, in the way that two very different creatures changed the shape of their world.

Oscar, of course, keeps flying. He always will. He says the air still has corners he hasn't seen yet.

And Eliana?

Well, she stays close. She's a connector now. A guide. She's the one the chipmunks come to when they start to wonder if there's more than just their tree and their tidy patch of ground.

She never pushes. She just smiles and says, "Maybe. Want to find out?"

And the sky? The sky is still open. It always was.

Every photo in this book shows a real place in and around Camden and Rockport. Can you spot them all?

Your Explorer's Checklist

Put a checkmark when you see these places in the photos or when you visit them in real life!

☐ Lilly Pond – Where Eliana first dreamed of adventure.
☐ Camden Harbor – Boats, schooners, and Oscar's favorite fishing spot.
☐ Rockport Harbor – Seals and sailboats in a quiet cove.
☐ Megunticook Lake – Shimmering waters beneath the mountains.
☐ Maiden Cliff – A soaring view where ospreys glide on the wind.
☐ Aldermere Farm – Rolling pastures and curious Belted Galloway cows.

Bonus Challenge

Keep your eyes open for Eliana's chipmunk cousins along the trails.
Listen carefully, can you hear Oscar's cry high above the trees?

Explorer's Safety Note

When you go out to find these places, always remember:

- Stay safe and be aware of your surroundings.
- Explore with a friend, family, or group, never alone.
- Bring water, snacks, and wear proper clothing and footwear for the outdoors.
- Watch the weather and plan ahead so your adventure stays fun and safe.

Adventure is best when you're prepared and together!

Discover More by J. Bramblewick

The adventures don't end here...

Explore more stories that bring the magic of Maine's harbors, lakes, and woodlands to life.

Look for more books to come in the future!

Keep exploring. Keep imagining. Keep reading.

Eliana has scampered over mossy stones by Lilly Pond.

Peeked from driftwood along the shore, and even tucked herself into grassy fields near Aldermere Farm.

Meanwhile, Oscar circles high above, keeping watch over the harbors, the lakes, and the winding forest trails.

When I first arrived in Maine, it was November. The air had already turned sharp and heavy with salt, and the harbors lay still beneath a quilt of fog and wind. The docks were empty, the boats pulled ashore, their hulls wrapped in white plastic like cocoons waiting for spring. It feltlike arriving at the end of something.

But endings, I would learn, have their own kind of beginning.

The days grew shorter. Nights stretched out, cold and starless. I lit candles in the evenings, wrapped myself in blankets, and found warmth in small rituals, a steaming cup of tea, a wool sweater pulled from the line, the creak of the old floorboards beneath my feet. Even in the depths of winter, I could smell the sea, faint and briny, like a ghost of summer carried on the wind. That scent reminded me that the ocean was never far, even when hidden beneath ice.

It was then I discovered Hygge (who-gah), the Danish word that captures a kind of quiet joy born from simplicity and closeness. It became my compass through winter, light the fire, be still, give thanks.

Gratitude started to mean something different to me. It wasn't about having more anymore, it was about seeing what was already right in front of me. The wind against the windows reminded me that warmth was a gift. And the deep, echoing quiet of a snow covered morning reminded me that even stillness has its own kind of life.

By late spring, the transformation was everywhere. The harbors came back to life almost overnight, men and women hauling out mooring lines, the thud of boots on wooden docks, laughter echoing over the cold harbor. Boats bobbed again in the current. Sailboats, lobster boats, kayaks, the coast awakening from its long sleep. The air grew warmer, and the briny scent returned, fuller now, alive with sunlight and seaweed and salt.

Then came summer, and with it, color. Lawns erupted in blossoms I couldn't name, lupines, wild roses and bergamot, growing thick along the roadside. The fields shimmered green under endless blue skies. Evenings stretched late into golden hours, the air soft and smelling faintly of pine and briny ocean spray. I thought of Florida then, the place I'd come from, all heat and sameness, and how here, every day felt like a page turning.

The locals jokingly complained when the temperature climbed into the eighties. I smiled quietly, remembering summers that never dipped below ninety-five. Gratitude again, in a different form, for cool air, for the laughter of neighbors, for ice cream dripping down my wrist in the sun.

And then, like clockwork, autumn arrived. The shift was instant, almost ceremonial. The air sharpened, the maples began to burn red and gold, and once again, the harbors filled with movement, this time in reverse. Boats hoisted out, shrink wrap pulled tight, docks lifted and stacked. Conversations lingered longer; everyone seemed to say goodbye to summer and to the rhythm that had carried us all year.

Jocularly, some said it was a sad time. And yet, I found peace in it. Because I understood now, the beauty of this place wasn't just in its color or its calm, but in its impermanence.

Winter came again. I watched the first snow fall on the same docks I'd seen bare a year before. The briny wind returned, faint but unmistakable, threading through the cold like a memory. I made a small fire, brewed tea, and smiled.

For the seasons that passed like breath.
For the people and places that change and return.
For the chance to be still long enough to notice it all.